To Angie and Jeff
With Best Wishes
Deb Chitwood

THE MAGIC RING

By Deb Chitwood

Illustrated by Stan Fraydas

POLESTAR PUBLICATIONS™

ISBN 0-942044-01-0
Published by:
POLESTAR PUBLICATIONS
620 South Minnesota Avenue
Sioux Falls, SD 57104
Library of Congress
Catalog Card Number: 82-62432

For all
who wish
to remember
how to use the
special gifts
they have
been given.

4

Here it is.
Here is your ring.
With this ring you can do anything.
And it will cost you not a thing.

You can bounce it.

Hold it.

Spin it.

Mold it.

Tie it in a knot.

Tie it in a bow.

Make beautiful music.

Play it high.

Play it low.

13

You can make people happy.
You can make people sing.
Oh, what wonderful things
You can do with your ring!

Or, you can make people sad.
You can make people mad.
But if you do that
You are being very, very bad.

You must use it for good
Or I'll take it away.
I'll take it away
Without delay.

And I'll keep it up here
While you get into your scrapes,
So it isn't bent into
More horrible shapes.

And then, when you're ready,
When you are much more aware
To love it
And feed it
And treat it with care,

I will give it
right back.

It was yours all along.
I am just here to protect it
So it isn't used wrong.

Oh, at times you may think,
"What a heavy, heavy weight.
Dragging this ring around I surely do hate."

But if you know the secret,
If you carry it just right,
It will not be heavy.
It will be light, light, light.

It will be so light
It will make you fly.
You can soar with it up to the sky.

And when you come down,
Lightly touching the ground,
You can bring people joy
           they may never have found.

Even better than that,
You know what to do
To help others find their forgotten rings too.

Oh, you may have to look closely.
Some rings may be so very small
That you will hardly be able to see them at all.

So find them
And feed them
And help them to grow
Healthy and strong and ready to go.

Then see them help others,
Find more people's rings,
Give everyone the joy
That the magic ring brings.

And soon there will be...

So many people
And so many rings
Doing so many wonderful, wonderful things!

ABOUT THE AUTHOR

Deb Chitwood is a native South Dakotan. She is the daughter of Glenn and Judy Arneson from Hayti, South Dakota. After receiving straight A's in both high school and college, Deb obtained her certification in Montessori education from the St. Nicholas Training Centre in London, England.

After teaching in Montessori schools in Iowa and Arizona, Deb began her own Montessori preschool in Sioux Falls, South Dakota, in August of 1980. She now directs her school, the Polestar Montessori School, and acts as a consultant for parents and early-childhood teachers.

Deb has been published in magazines and journals previously, but this is her first children's book. She is an accomplished musician who plays clarinet, recorder, piano, and guitar. She is presently working on her own poetry book as well as some other books with her author/psychologist husband, Dr. Terry Chitwood.